For Toni

CHARLES E. CARRYL

The Walloping Window-blind

ADAPTED AND ILLUSTRATED BY
JIM LAMARCHE

LOTHROP, LEE & SHEPARD BOOKS　　　NEW YORK

Library of Congress Cataloging in Publication

Carryl, Charles E. (Charles Edward), 1841-1920. The wallloping window-blind / by Charles E. Carryl; illustrations by Jim LaMarche. p. cm. Summary: An illustrated version of the nonsense poem about an extraordinary ship and the follies and misadventures of her madcap crew. ISBN 0-688-12517-4.—ISBN 0-688-12518-2 (lib. bdg.) 1. Children's poetry, American. [1. American poetry. 2. Nonsense verses.] I. LaMarche, Jim, ill. II. Title. PS1260.C65W3 1993 811'.4—dc20 92-40338 CIP AC

A capital ship for an ocean trip
    Was the *Walloping Window-blind*.
No gale that blew dismayed her crew
    Or troubled the captain's mind.

The man at the wheel was taught to feel
   Contempt for the wildest blow,
And it often appeared, when the weather had cleared,
   That he'd been in his bunk below.

The boatswain's mate was very sedate,
  Yet fond of amusement, too;
And he played hop-scotch with the starboard watch
  While the captain tickled the crew.

And the gunner we had was apparently mad,
For he stood on the cannon's tail,
And fired salutes in the captain's boots
In the teeth of a booming gale.

The captain sat in a commodore's hat
And dined in a royal way
On toasted pigs and pickles and figs
And gummery bread each day.

But the rest of us ate from an odious plate,
For the food that was given the crew
Was a number of tons of hot-cross buns
Chopped up with sugar and glue.

We all felt ill as mariners will
   On a diet that's cheap and rude,
And the poop deck shook when we dipped the cook
   In a tub of his gluesome food.

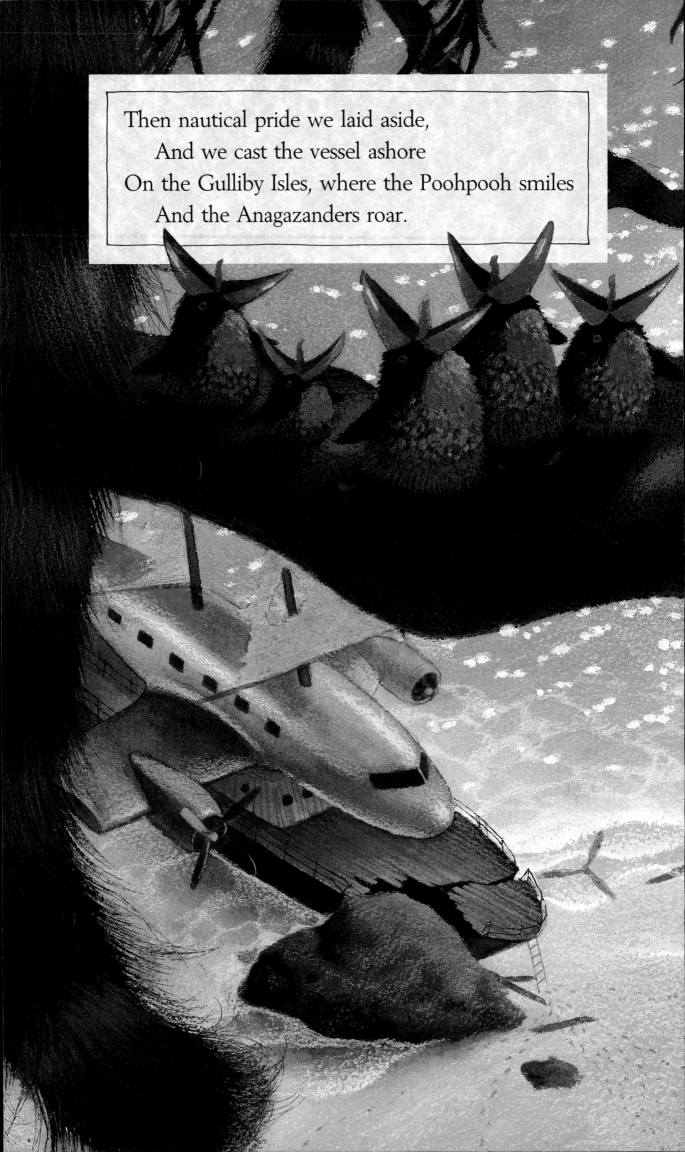

Then nautical pride we laid aside,
    And we cast the vessel ashore
On the Gulliby Isles, where the Poohpooh smiles
    And the Anagazanders roar.

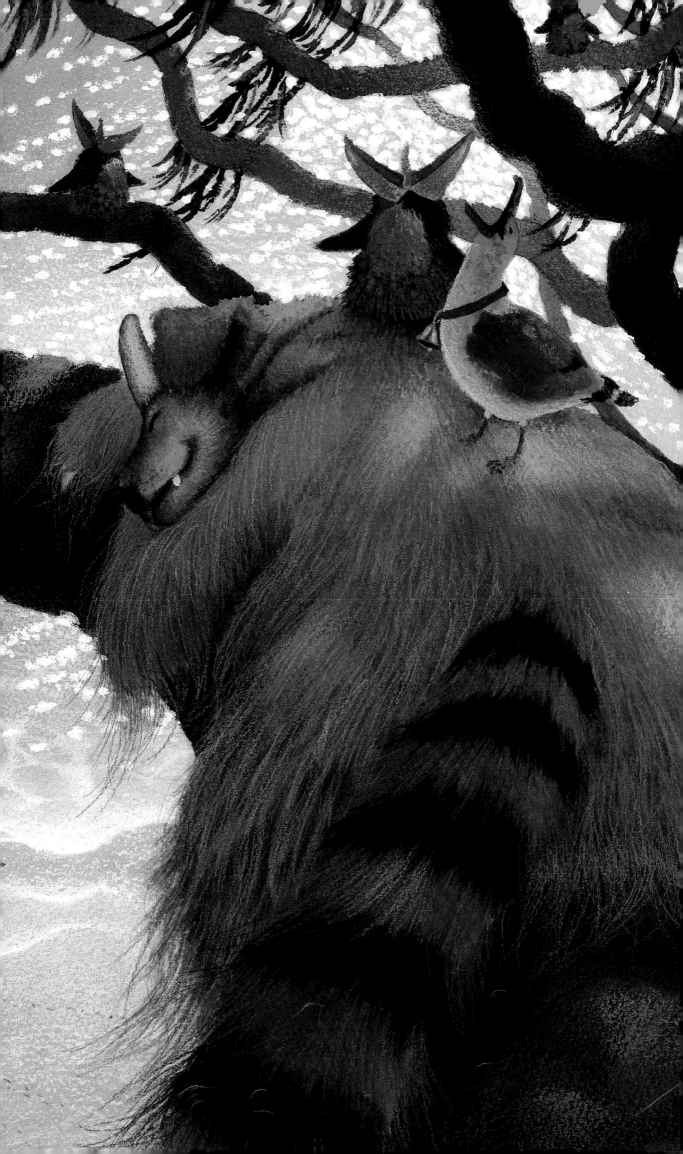

Composed of sand was that favored land,
  And trimmed with cinnamon straws;
And pink and blue was the pleasing hue
  Of the Tickletoeteaser's claws.

We climbed to the edge of a sandy ledge
  And soared with the whistling bee,
And we only stopped at four o'clock
  For a pot of cinnamon tea.

From dawn to dark, on rubagub bark
We fed, till we all had grown
Uncommonly thin. Then a boat blew in
On a wind from the torriby zone.

She was stubby and square, but we didn't much care,
    And we cheerily put to sea.
We plotted our course for the Land of Blue Horse,
    Due west 'cross the Peppermint Sea.